CW00839702

**Copyrigh**

First Edition

Dear Sue

Wishing you all the
best for your future

love

1

To Mum, Dad, and Dave you make my life richer in more ways than you could imagine.

In the end, there is only love.

# Spring

Hope Crescent belied its name. Thirty-nine semi-detached houses backing on to a scruffy field, called the 'Witching's'did little to enhance the neighbourhood. Built in the 1950's they shared a common identity, yet had nothing in common, the 1980's had seen to that. A bay window here, a porch, double glazing, and an old aluminium door, showed the residents need for individuality within their cloned world.

It's residents a rag bag of those who had failed to move and those looking for cheaper housing, aware that their aged homes were durable compared to the modern boxes of the day. Now with a new crisis, energy, the elderly and surviving population stood as relics of a post war and post prosperous era.

Ruth Bennet stood at an upstairs window, a mug of coffee gently steaming in her hand. Her eyes, as they always seemed to be these days were fixed on a single tree, another relic that had survived so many attempts at its destruction, whether from local hooligans or the council. This singe Sweet Chestnut tree survived and seemed to call out to Ruth, so much that she sometimes wouldn't come upstairs as its twisted, blackened, and bruised branches seemed to ensnare her mind. Dragging her eyes from the tree she stared at the garden. It had been wonderful once when Harry was alive.  Now it was a tangled mess of weeds instead of his neat, regimented borders of lobelia, pansies, and lavender.  They had all but died, and Ruth, not slovenly by nature had gradually let the garden go, as had most of her neighbours.

And like the tree, and untidiness of her garden alternatively mesmerised and taunted her.

The Reverend Dolores Lane straightened her back with a grunt. Stepping back, she surveyed the room critically. It would do, although she failed to understand why everyone assumed that vicars were fond of beige and brown.  Dolores loved colour, she always had, still at least her new cushions and books had given the room a more homely feel.

"Right!" She checked her watch again.  "Ten minutes before I need to leave." She added to no one in particular. Luckily the church was just across the road. I wouldn't do to be late on the first day.  Yawning she patted Lulu gently on the head and then gently massaged the blind German Shepherds silky soft fluffy ears as she quickly ran through her sermon.

New day, new dawn, new vicar, and a sermon which she hoped would start the day off on the right foot.

As the phone rang, Blaze, still anxious with her new surrounding barked her peculiar wheezing bark, a gentle if somewhat croaky 'woof' and the patter of feet heralded her bulky and somewhat clumsy entrance. Both puppies stared at Dolores, as they had when she'd swept into a rescue centre and swept back out again with a blind Lulu, a terrified Blaze who had been beaten and then tied to a tree and left to die, and three, of what she now considered demonic tortoiseshell cats called Verity, Madge, and Squirrel. The three terrors she knew where lurking under the kitchen table just waiting for an opportunity to ambush one of the dogs.

"Five minutes to go and you lot. You've got to behave." Pulling back her long black hair into a ponytail, she wandered into the hall hoping that she might find a hairband or at least an elastic band. Scrabbling about under the junk she'd dumped on the side, she found one and watched herself in an old blown mirror as she expertly tied her thick wayward hair into a subdued knot. Turning back to her animals she waved an admonishing finger at them.

"Behave or else!" She added with mock severity. She never raised her voice; the two dogs had had more than enough in their short lives. Watching their tails sink, they slunk back to their new beds in the kitchen, aware of the three tail swishing monsters, lurking under the table. Closing the door gently, she almost felt sorry for the two dogs, she could almost feel the cats rubbing their paws with glee as she walked down the hall!

Time to go!

Closing the front door, she gave herself a little nervous shake. At fifty she had swopped a life on stage, sex, drugs and rock 'n' roll for God, chastity, and gardening, and on the whole felt that her life was a whole better for it. OK she thought as she marched down the garden path to the front gate, she did still miss the sex and her old bandmates, but times and people changed and she had wanted something more, besides at fifty she felt that the new videos she was supposed to make humiliating. Who wanted to see a woman her age gyrating her hips and trying to pull guys half her age. Yanking the old, warped gate open she added yet another job to her to do list. The modern comfortable house she had been originally offered had disappeared into the ether, and she was left with a house that she knew if she wasn't careful, could love.

Ruth was also aware that she was late as she hurried up the street, her heels pit patting in an uneven rhythm, her ankles protesting at being forced into high heels. Her dreams that night had haunted her. She'd been in a church that she didn't recognise, and someone there, in a loud voice had been lecturing her about gardening, and now for the first time since Harry's death she was going to church.

Lulled by the softness of the church, Dolores began to relax. Not too bad a turn out. They'd all come to gawp, but she was used to that. She'd been unashamed of her choice of hymns, having ignored the hymn selection she was supposed to choose from. She liked ones that people knew and could sing to, good school assembly ones. As her voice floated up to the rafters, she could hear the three in the front trying to outdo each other, a rather lovely bass coming from the back and a fair smattering of octaves that seesawed their way across the notes as they dipped and rose a fraction of a beat behind the others. She loved it.

Ruth had been surprised. Father Patrick had gone and in his stead was this angel voiced woman. Her accent soft and unidentifiable gave the words a whole new meaning. She could feel the words, they thrilled her. She was aware that the others too were listening, really listening.

"And so, when I think of Eden, I don't think of it as a place we were locked out of, I see Eden as a place that we were supposed to create." Lifting her eyes slowly, Dolores assessed her congregation, they were listening, she could already feel it. The twitchiness had gone, the church had taken on a feeling of peace of those within it. Smiling she went on "God gave us the blueprint, and whether or not we wanted to live in blessed ignorance, isn't really what is at stake here. It's what we do with the plans. Gardens, I think are a reflection of our souls. Gardens and souls can be rigid and regimented; untidy, neglected gardens, that contain so much promise, and my favourite," pausing and swallowing down her passion, she steadied her voice "community gardens where plants are encouraged to grow and support one another, and that is how we should think of our communities, as gardens. Not singular, regimented, but soft, yielding, and supportive, so that we all have a chance of growing and being able to have the right nutrients so that we can become strong and help one another. God strove to create perfection, God is perfection. We are not, neither is nature. But when you open your front or back door what do you see? A wonderous beauty that you are blessed to be a part of, or a chore you would rather leave for another day?

When I garden, I feel close to God. He created our planet, our world. He shared his amazing blueprint with us, and even when I do something as simple as a little weeding, planting, pricking the first beans I feel a sense of wonder, and an even larger sense of God's power and benevolence." Dolores inner child squeaked and applauded. Dolores could feel them, for that moment if she had cried "let's storm that awful little café down the road and demand better coffee," they would have followed her. She could still feel the gritty granules sticking to her teeth. She'd popped in on her way back from her interview and had vowed never to go back!

Dolores, waiting in the porch, felt that the blood was squeezed from her hand, as one by one everyone said their thanks, they'd all been a little shy of her.

"That was so beautiful!" Ruth could feel herself clutching at Dolores hands as she left "I feel I want to go home and mow the lawn and do a thousand and one other things."

Laughing, Dolores gently teased her. "You don't need to do quite so many, just do one. Something that you know will give you pleasure. Do you enjoy gardening?"

"I..I" Ruth hesitated, feeling her face flush with anxiety. "I used to, but Harry, that's my husband, he's dead" she blurted out, "he didn't think I was very good and did it himself. He was very good," she added earnestly, "he liked Lobelia and pansies." Aware of the people behind her, Ruth blushed, her face puckering with embarrassment, that she dropped Dolores hand quickly. "I'm sorry, I'm taking up too much of your time."

"Not at all. Pop round and have a chat. Perhaps, we can rekindle your love of gardening again." Smiling her impish smile, she allowed Ruth to move on and started talking to Ted Butcher, the owner of Butcher's Greengrocer and general store. All the time she was talking she was aware that Ted's focus was keenly fixed on Ruth's retreating figure. A romance? Possible, not nothing yet, as far as she had been aware they had not said anything or even looked at each other during the service. But perhaps potential for the future.

Walking quickly, Ruth was just about to pass Ted's shop when a display of Polyanthus caught her attention. She had loved them, Harry had not. With their bright hues of yellow, red, and purple, Ruth felt that a rainbow had just come out on the drab side of the street. She was about to pass on, but suddenly halted. Why couldn't, or why shouldn't she buy them. Just staring at them brought a sense of happiness. It was then Dolores words popped into her head, "what do you see when you open your back door." Her heart lurched for a second. She saw nothing, just a barren emptiness. Automatically she picked out the three yellow Polyanthus and was just about to step into the shop when Ted came up behind her. Been trying to shift them all week. Tell you what, if you buy those, I'll give you the other three as a present. How about that?"

Goggling at her father's sudden generosity, Maggie Butcher, stared at him as he handed her three pots of blooms. Been trying to shift them all week! The laughter bubbled up inside her. They'd only arrived yesterday, and these were all they had left. Soft her dad was, soft. Well soft where Ruth was. Maggie had caught him watching her when she'd popped in for some milk last week. Dad was lonely and Ruth was a nice woman, a little browbeaten but when she smiled, even she had felt its charm and warmth. And yes, it was time her father found someone else. Mum had been dead for ten years; it was time he moved on.

Clutching her purchases, Ruth sped home, her feet no longer pinching in her tight shoes. She knew where she would put them. And yet, as she entered the house she felt its enervating presence, that before she knew it, she had left her shopping on the kitchen table, made herself a cup of coffee and a sandwich and was now mesmerised by a cat loving YouTuber.

A couple of days later Dolores was whistling in the greenhouse, snatches of song which danced and weaved through her brain as she scribbled a chord, a couple of notes, or words that tantalised and teased her. Brushing her hair from her face, forgetting that her hands were covered in soil she felt peaceful. When she'd left the band, she'd sworn that she would never write again. That had lasted, what two years. Within weeks of becoming priested and having her own parish, she'd written and sold a song to a young pop princess. The royalties had helped pay for the renovation of the church tower. A new parish and a new song, this time it had paid for the church hall and vicarage improvements, and now a third song floated in front of her eyes, and yes, she already knew what she would do with this one. This time, it would be a community project and she knew exactly what it was.

The only thing that had initially disturbed her equanimity was Gavin. Gavin had appeared three days ago at her door, suitcase in hand clearly thinking she was expecting him. He was her new curate. Father Patrick had organised it all. Her problem, and she considered it her problem was that Gavin was high church, and she thought she was about as low as you could go. She loved God but didn't like him dressed up. She had always sworn that she would teach good sound Anglicism, that would help people, give them both strength and courage. She had to admit, she felt slightly intimidated by him. What was worse, was that he was two years older than her and towered above her. And now her barren house was becoming a home.

Besides Gavin, she had hired a cleaner, Mrs T. Mrs T or Trebber, like Gavin had arrived out of the blue, soaked to the skin having cycled the five miles in the rain from her home to the vicarage on the off chance that Dolores may need someone to look after the house.

Reading between the lines, Dolores realised that the woman was desperate.

"I'm sure they wouldn't mind me coming out for a couple of hours a day, that's my children," she'd replied, her hands knotting in her lap as she said the words. "I mean I can cook, clean and look after the children as well." Her rabbity teeth pinched her lower lip as she spoke, her eyes not quite meeting Dolores, as she bit into a piece of chocolate cake that she'd been given. Three cups of tea later, Dolores decided to employ her, but it was a live in post only. The house was huge and meant for a large Victorian family, not one vicar and her five monstrous pets. Only yesterday Blaze had pinched a pair of Gavin's underpants off the drier and run down the path with them, much to the amusement of her two churchwardens, Viv and Terry. Gavin hadn't seemed quite so amused!

"Live in?" Dolores watched as the other woman cowered slightly in the chair. Blaze who had wandered into the room, sat down at her feet, surprising Dolores, Blaze was nervous of other people and usually hid.

"Well Blaze likes you. So, all you have to do is say yes and tell me when you want to start."

Instead of replying, Mrs T burst into tears, her hands shaking as she tried to stem the tide. "I'm…"

"Would you like Gavin to come and help you pick up your things." Yes, she thought, Gavin would be ideal, at 6.4 he would loom over any objectors. They weren't to know that he was the gentlest soul alive. Like Mrs T she had been quick to realise that Gavin was initially unsure about working for a woman vicar.

He still was. But it worked; the cats bullied Gavin out of his breakfast in the morning. Slices of bacon disappeared from his plate to the fiends below, and if not that, Squirrel had a habit of headbutting his spoon out of the way and dunking her nose into his breakfast cereal. Blaze adored Mrs T and followed her around the house, and here she was, in her greenhouse with Lulu lying on a piece of old sacking, her sightless eyes staring adoringly at Dolores.

"Hello!" Jumping Dolores immediately reached out for Lulu who turned and barked at the stranger.

"Lulu quiet." Touching the dog's nose with a finger, Lulu sat. It was a totally new ball game teaching a dog touch language.

"Hi, don't worry about Lu. Come on in."

Offering her hand first for Lulu to sniff, Ruth stepped into Dolores inner sanctum.

"I was hoping you would call in for a chat. Do you mind if I just finish pricking out these beans and then I'll rustle up a pot of coffee."

"If you're…"

"I'm never too busy. I've spent a lifetime being besieged by people. Unlike most, I love it. Lu," she touched the dog's head this time, pushing her finger softly against her head. Lu, assured that there was no threat, moved back onto her sacking bed and sighed, while her eyes flickered between the two women.

"So," asked Dolores as she began to sift potting compost into a series of pots, "what would you like to talk about?"

"Mmmm" Ruth stuttered, she had rehearsed what she would like to say and now found that the words had dried up in her throat.

"Eden?"

Dolores nodded, concentrating on sifting the soil gently and evenly across a batch of battered yoghurt pots.

"You said that gardens were often a reflection of our souls."

"I do, for like gardens souls need be maintained, left to rot and redeemed again. We have the power for so much growth, just like a garden."

"So, it's never too late?"

"To late for what?"

"To plant a new garden?"

Pausing with her hands in mid-air, soil clinging to her fingers holding a seedling with the care and love of a parent, Dolores smiled softly, the corners of her mouth, curving into a smile that had seduced millions of men into thinking her one of the sexiest women alive.

"We always have time to plant a new garden for ourselves. The trouble is that we get in our own way and say we can't do it before we even try."

"It does seem exhausting. I bought these flowers; Ted even gave me some and yet I somehow cannot find the energy to plant them." Ruth's laugh was tinged with haunting undertones. Dolores could feel her sadness and her apathy.

"That's what I mean. We get in our own way, because I bet you feel that you have to do the whole garden just for these few plants."

Ruth nodded.

"Well of course you'll feel overwhelmed. I feel overwhelmed with this garden. So much needs doing, fences to be painted and fixed, the lawn needs reseeding, its massive. But instead of worrying about it I'm in here planting seedlings because that is all I can do today." Dusting her hands off with an old towel she picked up a watering can and began to delicately water her seedlings. "If there is one thing I have learned and that's to take baby steps. Because each step you take, whether big or small is progress. You bought the plants, that's progress. When you go home think about where you would like to plant them. Imagine them in all their glory. And then, instead of thinking you have to dig, mow and tidy the whole garden. Take on a small patch that you can deal with.  It's like life. Don't take on the whole thing, just do today what you can manage, and tomorrow you may be able to do a little more.  All you need to do is start, you've taken the first step, the hardest step of all.  Now all you need to do is allow yourself to take a baby step every day, and if that doesn't happen, don't beat yourself up about it."

"You make it sound so simple." Ruth's voice held a tinge of regret.

"It is if you allow it to be.  The trouble is we human's love complicating things.  Me, I am what I am, and I do what I can. That's all that God has ever asked of me.  He feels the same way about you.  All he wants us to do, is live our best lives.  He doesn't care about what car you drive, where you live or how much money you have in your bank account.  He wants you to live, so allow yourself to live a little." She watched as Ruth's brows contracted, her brown eyes flickering like that of a frightened rabbit. "Come on, I've been a bit too straight forward. Let's have that coffee."

Later that evening, Ruth brushed the soil from her knees.  Dolores had been right.  Just take a simple step. The polyanthus now lay snug alongside a path.  Even on a dreary overcast day they shone with promise, colour and for the first time, she thought love. Sitting down on a small wall, she let the trowel rest against an old Lavender stump, drew her knees up to her chest and smiled. Instead of castigating herself over the state of the garden she started looking at it with new eyes. The path and straight borders were boring, in her mind's eye she began to soften the borders, she could see herself walking down a meandering path to the back gate which opened out onto the field. If she painted the fences a soft sage green she would open the garden up, blur the borders that had held her prisoner. Suddenly she laughed, hugging her knees she suddenly felt alive. She could do this!

Later that night, instead of ignoring the tree, she stared at it. She couldn't believe it, for the first time since she had moved there was the hint of blossom hidden within its branches.

Three days later, Ruth knocked at the vicarage front door. Trying not to look disappointed, she stared at Gavin's tartan bedroom slippers.

"Sorry"

"Don't worry about it. Both Dolores and Mrs T are out so the cats and I were having a little me time."

"Me time?"

"That's the cats, I was trying to write but Madge feel asleep on my keyboard, and I didn't want to move her." He added sheepishly. Ruth's smile matched his. "Oh, I am pleased you called, Dolores thought you would. She's got some plants for you."

"For me?"

"Yes, come on through. She's left them in the conservatory."

Following Gavin, through the quiet hallway, Ruth couldn't believe that Dolores had given up her life for this. Photos of her beamed down from the walls, platinum discs held pride of place and yet, the house like its new tenant seemed oblivious to the fame and fortune attached to her.

"Makes you think, doesn't it. All this" Gavin swept his hand along the wall "And she gave it all up."

"She found her calling."

"Yes." Gavin turned and smiled his odd humorous smile "I think she has. She really believes. I've never met anyone who treats God as if he is her best friend."

"It must be very different?"

"It is, it's different from everything I have ever known or been taught. I must admit I was worried when I came here. Father Patrick was high church, and I thought that was what I wanted."

"And now?"

"I think, no I know, I want to understand him like Dolores does. It's the way she explains him, takes away all the mystic and talks about him in such a way that I feel him enter my soul. I want to be able to inspire people like she does."

"You think she does" Asked Ruth as they walked through a comfy if untidy lounge into an old conservatory filled with boots, dog baskets, cat toys and a wooden carving of a man kneeling in supplication before an unseen God. The honey tones of the wood called out to her, as her hand drifted towards it, Gavin said.

"You feel it too. Dolores calls him Arthur. Someone made him for her, and she loves him." Sweeping her hands over the carvings head, Ruth couldn't believe how tactile and soft the wood felt under her fingers. He felt warm, alive, vibrant! The unseen eyes and calm face bent in prayer. Her fingers strayed over its narrow yet strong shoulders. The wood felt like flesh under her tentative fingers, it yielded, it felt so soft that she could almost imagine rolling and massaging the flesh softly between her fingers. Gavin smiled at her as she blushingly snatched her hand away from him.

"Don't worry about it, he gets us all like that. The Church Council were in awe of him, and if it wasn't for Dolores personality, I think they would have all been talking to him. Ah, here we go."

Picking up an old fruit container, Gavin smiled at her look of shock.

"There are so many!"

"She wasn't sure about what you wanted or liked. So, I think she's thrown in half the greenhouse. The ones at the back," he motioned with his head, his eyes still gently fixed on Ruth are all vegetables. Tomatoes, beans, and lettuce. The rest are flowers, she did tell me what they were, but I can't remember, although I do think she mentioned sunflowers at some point. Would you like me to carry them for you. You look a little shell shocked."

"Shell shocked, I don't know where to begin or even how to pay her."

"Oh, that's simple. She said plant them with love, and then when they grow and once you have eaten enough, share the rest with your neighbours."

"Neighbours?"

"Thar's what she said. Come on we'll walk through the back garden. Give you an idea of what to expect, although she did say that you need to keep them all indoors for a little longer to avoid the frosts."

"I'm still trying to get my head around neighbours. We don't speak to each other. Perhaps the odd nod but we've never been what you call a friendly street."

"Well then, 'it's time for a change. They reached the garden gate at the same time as Ted, he'd heard their voices and unaware of the slither of jealousy that entered his heart, had stopped.

"Morning Ted. Dolores has just given Ruth what appears to be half a tonne of seedlings, I don't suppose you would help her carry them home? I promised to call in at Mrs Lancombe's this morning and"

"No, I can take Ruth home. Interjected Ted quickly, not wishing to hear about Mrs Lancombe's latest adventures with the NHS.

"Splendid. Ruth it was lovely to see you this morning, and Ted I was wondering, I need a couple of new drill bits, could I pop in this afternoon and have a look at what you've got."

"Course, if I'm not there Maggie will, and she knows the DIY section as well as any man."

"Thanks," and then looking at Ruth "call again soon."

Handing Ruth's precious burden over to Ted, Gavin watched them go, a beam of mild amusement crossing his face. Dolores had been right. There was something between them, yet neither of them knew it. Love, yes that what was needed, a little love. Watching them disappear, he lit a forbidden cigarette and waited for

Lulu to join him, flopping down, she rolled inelegantly on her back and demanded a tummy rub.

"You, young lady are a time waster. Tickling her chin, he grinned into her wide mouth grin, tongue lolling as she wiggled with pleasure. Dolores, he thought had a knack of making the mundane, the sad and the lonely feel whole again. Deciding against a personal visit, he lit another cigarette, before dialling Mrs Lancombe's number. He hadn't really promised to call round, he'd said he'd be in touch. Lowering himself down onto one of the rickety garden chairs with Lulu at his feet, the feel of a cigarette between his fingers he dialled the number, knowing full well that Mrs T had spied him and that within minutes a mug of tea and a slice of fruit cake would appear as if by magic. Even God he thought would have needed a couple of minutes to prepare himself from the onslaught of Mrs L and the 'ruddy useless NHS!"

The silence between Ted and Ruth was companionable and tinged with a little nervousness. Tongue-tied and a little uncomfortable, they choose easy silence.

Finally, unable to control himself any longer Ted asked, "What are you going to do with all this stuff?"

Ruth paused before answering, her first thought would be to throw them in the bin and say they had perished. However! Even her own answer surprised her, "plant them. I think" she suddenly turned around and looked at him. "I think….I think I'm going to redesign the garden, and these are going to help me. Dolores asked me to give any produce I can't eat away. And suddenly, I think it's a wonderful idea. I don't even know who my neighbours are. We never talk, we never see each other."

"Yeah, well don't put me out of business." Retorted Ted gruffly, as his hands tightened under the now buckling weight of the plants.

"I don't think that will happen, but just image how you'd feel if someone."

"Dumped their unwanted veg on your drive."

"I didn't mean it like that!" Ruth's voice dropped to a whisper, her fingers suddenly clutching at her coat buttons as they had when Harry had told her she was stupid, and unable to cope without him.

The silence changed. Ted could feel it. Cursing himself for being so brutal and unfeeling, he ventured softly "You'll probably have more for more than just one neighbour, perhaps I could have some. People are always asking when their veg is grown and I know a little farm shop in Harlingdon which is desperate for good quality veg. Perhaps you could help them as well?"

A couple of women pushed past with prams, ignoring them they walked on, their feet beating a steady tattoo on the pavement.  Ted and Ruth walked on. It wasn't until they turned the corner towards, the house that Ruth finally spoke.

"That would be a lovely idea.  Shall we see how things grow.  I've not really gardened for years, so it'll be a bit hit and miss.  But all of a sudden, instead of seeing a garden of weeds I feel I could make a difference. Does that seem stupid to you?"

Shaking his head, Ted muttered softly "No, and I'm sorry about back then.  I was talking out of turn.  You grow your vegetables, and if you need any help just give me a shout.  In fact, between you and me, I might have a go at growing some meself and then we could swop.

"You mean barter?" Asked Ruth, her voice vibrating with surprise.

"Why not.  No one's got any money. Old Mr Digby, he still grows veggies, perhaps he'd want to help us."

Ruth could feel the excitement tingling through her body. She felt alive, the enervating shawl that she had been dragging around with her for years, slipped slightly off her shoulders, as she caught a glimpse of herself being part of something.  She'd felt so hurt for so long that she was now too afraid to give, but…."

Ted also felt the change, her walk became lighter, her often bowed head had found the strength to hold itself high. Smiling to himself, he hitched the plants a little higher, more to relieve his aching arms than anything else and, matching her stride walked confidently beside her.

Despite the awkward goodbye at the gate, Ruth felt happy. Walking into the house she switched the kettle on, but instead of reaching for the TV remote control to escape into Poirot's gentile world of splendour and murder, she went upstairs and changed. Moving from room to room she opened windows, picked up clothes, books, newspapers and trivia that she had walked past and ignored for the last eighteen months. Staring at the house with new eyes, she realised that Dolores words, also referred to her home. Was this how she saw her soul, untidy, empty, funless, and bland? No, she wasn't going to stay inside, she needed to be in the garden, it was still too early to plant out, but she could at least get them ready in the greenhouse and clear the borders along the fence.

Shaking her shoulders, she could feel a little defiance creeping into her soul, she'd change them for a start, add curves, make them bigger. The lawn had stood between her and her wish to go out for a drive on a Sunday afternoon. Harry always mowed the lawn, whether it needed it or not, taking a spade and digging a great fat hole in it would give her infinite pleasure she decided.

Driving home, Dolores wondered what had made her do this. She had sold her piano, put her three vintage guitars in storage and had promised herself that music, or her music, was behind her. It was still a temptation, a little worm that burrowed in her soul, flickered at the back of her mind and just when she thought she'd got the better of it, it was there. Talking to her, lifting her heart with notes so pure she could hardly breathe, and now, sitting on the back seat was an electronic piano. She hated keyboards, yet a new Yamaha nestled inside its box, tantalising and tempting. She could hardly wait, the feel of piano keys under her fingertips, and not the old, battered thing in the church which she was determined to replace. OK it was not a grand, she had sold hers, vicarages and grand pianos didn't go and her parishioners of her two inner city parishes would not have confided or taken her to their hearts knowing who she was or what she owned; besides she thought as she slowed down for a horse and rider, the bloody thing would have been nicked!

For two houses at least, that Sunday afternoon, was filled with the noise of huffing and puffing. Ruth could hardly feel her arms, even lifting the mug of coffee made her left arm muscles tremble, perspiration glistened on her face alongside a streak of mud and the whisps of dust from an old potting compost bag. Ignoring her aching body, Ruth couldn't believe what she had achieved. Already, the section of the garden she'd been working on, had taken on a new life, a fresher wholesome look. She'd found an old compost bin at the back of the garden and with the aid of a hammer, baling twine and her new best friends – brute, force, and ignorance – had managed to get it to resemble something it had been designed to do. She'd enjoyed littering the lawn, ignoring the mental keep off the grass signs and had cut into its wispy turf with a nice sharp blade. The sheer anarchy of it had made her laugh. Lifting her face to the sudden shards of sunshine which darted in and out of the clouds, Ruth sighed and suddenly felt at peace.

Dolores was not feeling particularly peaceful, she had a sudden need for noise, the beat of drums, the torn-out chords of a guitar and she wanted her bandmates. All of a sudden, a Sunday afternoon of jamming would have soothed her soul. She felt excited, adrenalin seemed to course through her veins, she couldn't sit still and as much as she had promised herself that she would settle down and use the afternoon to catch up on her admin, the song kept haunting her. Even now, while she was staring at an email from Viv, the words had disappeared and turned into notes. She could hear the music, the beat of the drum, snatches of music burst in on her, and to her left lay her notepad with a dozen scrawled lines on it.

The song would work, she knew that.  She always did. When the music and lyrics fell out of her brain and onto the page, she knew it was a hit.  The moment she tried to write or contrive to write something she thought she should write, it was doomed.  Half written lyrics littered her music boxes, notepads burgeoning with potential lay, dusty and rotting at the bottom of cupboards. These were the failures, the ones that would never see the light of day.  Every musician had them, they were a bit like exotic plants, no matter how hard you tried they didn't thrive, her soul was missing from them. 'We met in the city of Angels, where the sky kissed the earth." She could see them, a couple, Adam and Eve? Ignoring the computer, she walked over to the study window and stared outside.  The sun was finally coming out, and the garden, with its bright hues glowed.  Staring she could hear the rest of the lyrics "Two hearts meeting, two hearts beating."

Humming softly, she turned to her new piano.  Half an hour wouldn't make any difference, and who really expected a vicar to work on a Sunday afternoon?  Gavin was out and Mrs T was having afternoon tea and Scrabble at the Fosdykes.  Switching it on, she could feel the thrill deepen inside her, as her fingers gently brushed the notes.  Pulling her phone out of her pocket she set it to record and slowly began to let the notes in her head reach down into her fingertips and she softly began to play, lost in a dream where the words painted pictures that flittered and floated inside her brain, a kaleidoscope of images and notes.

As she began to sing a richness filled the air, both Blaze and Lulu snuggled up together on an old rug, snoring happily while the kittens, tired after chasing butterflies in the garden, settled down on top of them. Blaze snorted once, wriggled, and drifted off into a deep sleep, and all the while, Dolores voice caressed the bricks and mortar of the room, rubbing off its old patina and like the animals, allowing it to take on a new feeling of peace and harmony.

# Summer

Spring turned into Summer and Ruth couldn't get over the change in her. Afternoons in front of the TV were a distant memory. She loved her garden; it had become her sanctuary. OK after two visits to A & E, once for stabbing her eye on a twig and the second for skewering her hand with a nail, she had bought a book on DIY. Ted had said he would help her, but she was afraid to ask for too much. Besides when he came over, he seemed to enjoy pottering about her garden and drinking tea, rather than doing any actual work.

She loved the smell of tomatoes on the vine, standing there in the greenhouse she inhaled their heady scent. There was a lot to be done, she had dug up the early potatoes, carrots and beetroot. The come and cut again spicy lettuces waved tantalisingly at her. She had grown to love their peppery flavours and had even started coming out late at night, not only to smell the heady scent of stocks, nicotina and rose, but to deter the little brute's intent on eating her bounty. The parish lantern, Dolores had called it, and even now, at the end of the day, she found herself wandering out into the garden in her pyjamas, carrying her customary mug of tea, a biscuit, and sitting on the little rock seat by the pool she watched the moon and the bats as they swooped and dived across her garden, gobbling up insects, creating a frenzied yet orchestrated activity of their own.

And like her garden, the Sweet Chestnut tree bloomed, nodding its branches in the gentle breeze. Ruth had never felt peaceful, content or so happy.

Honouring her promise, that evening she bagged up potatoes, carrots, and tomatoes. She wasn't sure how she was going to do this. She didn't know her neighbours, but since her gardening adventures she had met them on a more regular basis. They like her seemed interested in the garden and had been particularly enthusiastic when she asked if they would mind if she pulled the Leylandii hedging out and installed a wood panelled fence. She wanted more room, and those monsters seemed to drain the garden of moisture and life. It had been worth it, the new fence, painted a soft sage green so create an illusion that the garden was bigger, had been her biggest investment and the most transformative. She was no longer oppressed by their size and thuggishness. And now the time had come; to honour her promise.

She knew they worked late. Should she call or just leave the vegetables with a little note? Ted had said that they would probably be insulted and suggested that she give him her overspill. At first, she had been tempted, it would be so much easier to give to him, yet at the back of her mind she could her Dolores voice. The need for community, for people to start talking again, Technology hadn't brought people together, it had driven them apart. People couldn't communicate unless it was via a screen. No, she would go next door, ring the bell and if no one answered, she would leave the parcel on their front doorstep with a note. What was the worst that could happen? If they didn't like them, they could give them back.

It wasn't until she walked out of her front gate that she felt sick. What if they laughed at her, mocked her, or told her that they didn't want her charity. It was all she could do not to run back into the safety of her house, but no, she had made a promise and she was going to stick to it.

Timidly ringing the doorbell Ruth took a step back, she couldn't believe it, even the backs of her legs were shaking. There were no lights on, but she waited a minute to give them time. Finally, realising that there was no one home, she left the carrier bag of vegetables by the door, a hastily pre-written note attached to the handle, saying that she hoped they would enjoy them.

Sighing with relief, she scuttled back to her house, quickly closing the door.

For two days, Ruth felt nothing but disappointment, the carrier bag had gone but no message had been posted through her door. Feeling slightly peeved, she took her frustrations out on the slugs that were making a beeline for her newly planted Hosta's.

Having managed to escape the fiends, who had of late insisted on coming out and walking with the dogs, making a twenty-minute walk feel like a lifetime as they explored every nook and cranny that the dogs sniffed, chased their tails and were, the most incredible timewasters, hooligans, and comedians that she'd ever met. Dolores felt relieved she had managed to leave them at home and decided to walk them through the Witching's. The place annoyed her, the whole street annoyed her, its grimy downtrodden look, battered gardens and equally battered populous.

The field was a mess, littered with old bicycles, nettles, beer bottles and unmentionable dank and squidgy things, Dolores silently walked with the dogs. Keeping both by her side, they ambled amiably. Despite the poor setting, the tree looked better now than it had when she'd first moved in. Perhaps it was the rain, or perhaps it always looked ragged before it turned its tears into splendour.

As she walked on a back gate of one of the houses opened and out stepped Ruth. Waving to each other, Dolores gently padded towards the other woman.

"It gets you too?" Ruth's voice was unsteady, unsure of the words she was speaking, her hands tucked away in her jean's pockets, trembled slightly.

"Yes, but I think in a different way." Slipping off Blaze's lead, she allowed the puppy to bound over to Ruth, Lulu whining, strained at her leash. Gently correcting her, Dolores moved closer so that Lulu also felt Ruth's presence.

"In what way?" Asked Ruth her face buried in Blaze's thick fluffy fur, sneezing suddenly as the fur tickled her nose, Blaze shot off, zooming around them madly. Lulu desperate to play cried and yelped so that Dolores, checking there were no other dogs around let her off to bumble after Blaze. Blaze, she knew would slow down for Lulu and play with her in the untidy grass.

"Me," Dolores pursed her lips and thought for a moment, rocking back onto her right foot, her left gently tapping the ground. "I suppose, I see trees as towers of strength, of new hope and life." Smiling she added "They outlive us, support, and protect us. They are a bit like God I suppose, they do so much for us and yet we abuse their gentle and powerful nature. Take this one for example, people have cut into its wood, tried to burn it alive, battered it, torn limbs from it, and yet its leafy canopy protects us from the heat, it provides structure and stability for the soil, it breathes what we cannot breathe and yet gives us oxygen to sustain ourselves. Trees are wonderous, magnificent, and I cannot help but being in awe of them." Laughingly, she added "I know, I'm mad!"

Laughing with her, Ruth's words surprised the other woman "not mad, but you are unusual!"

"Lifetime in music babe!" Throwing her arms out theatrically she twirled around "Do you know it's done me good to be out here in this miserable little field and talking to you. My brain's cleared. I was getting bogged down, so many distractions. Don't get me wrong, I'm lucky, I have Gavin and he works his socks off."

Hesitantly, Ruth asked "would you like to come in and have a cup of tea, you can see my new garden.

"Love to, but are you sure you haven't got anything stronger than tea?"

"Coffee or a twenty-year-old bottle of Tequila."

"You devil, you!" laughed Dolores before whistling for the dogs to come to heel. "Clipping on Lulu's lead she added "I think I'll settle for the tea!"

Walking back home along the street, thinking of the change she had noticed in Ruth, both puppies now tired, walking soberly at her heels, she was surprised when a face popped up behind a hedge.

"Hello, how are you?" She added breezily, slowing down to give the other person time to say hello.

"You that new gardening vicar up at St. Matthews?"

"Yes, that me. Dolores Lane and you are?"

"Peter, Peter Downey." Wiping his hands on his jacket he offered her a mud encrusted hand. Shaking it firmly, Dolores added.

"Nice to meet you, what a beautiful dog rose."

"Used to be, full of blooms. These days I'm lucky if I just get one or two. Going to dig it out and leave it just as a bare wall," he muttered.

"Oh! That would be such a shame. Staring at its untidy mess, she went on boldly "What if I came and gave you a little bit of help with it. It's really too early to prune, but if we cut out the dead wood, re-train it, feed and water it, we could give it one more chance to look wonderful again."

"You'd do that?"

"Yes."

"And what do you want from me?" He added roughly "I'm not coming to church."

"You don't have to." Dolores bit her tongue. Why did everyone have to be so defensive? She so hated this new world of built-in aggression.

Peter stood there chewing his lips, his fingers drumming a tattoo against his faded corduroy trousers. Torn between hacking out his frustrations on the rose bush or having some company for a couple of hours while they tidied it up."

"Alright! When?"

Pausing for a moment to think, trust her to suggest something during her busiest week. "How about Friday afternoon, 4 pm?"

"Sure, you can spare the time?" Came the sneering answer.

"Fine." Counting silently under her breath as she walked away.

"Oi, wait up. I didn't say I couldn't make it. Four you say?"

Dolores heard the desperation in his voice. Turning around, staring him straight in the eye, she nodded.

"Right see you then." Although the words were gruff, Dolores could feel the relief underneath. Waving her goodbye, she walked slowly home.

The dogs tired from their walk, drank noisily from their bowls, and settled down by the open patio doors in the music room. This was her den, the only room everyone else was banned from. She'd moved her office desk into an alcove and decided that this was her inner space. Her place to get away from the world.

Popping his head through the open door, Gavin muttered "You look knackered! Want a coffee?"

"Wouldn't mind something a little stronger." Dropping wearily into a chair, tilting her head back she yawned. What a day! But perhaps a very successful one.

Ruth stared at the note and jar of pickled beetroot that sat on her front step, tears were flooding down her face. It was from her next-door neighbours.

*Dear Ruth,*

*Thank you for the vegetables and sorry for not writing sooner to say thank you for your well-timed gift. Life has been a bit difficult recently.*

*I'm sorry that we aren't able to give you anything back, but my mother-in-law has made you some pickled beetroot from the ones you gave us and hopes that you will enjoy it*

*Once again, thank you for your generosity. It really made our day.*

*Sarah*

Dolores had been right. Communities had been eroded by technology; it was time to start bringing them back to life again.

As the weeks moved on, a subtle change came over Hope Crescent. It was hardly noticeable at first.

Twitching curtains had given way to nosiness as the Vicar of St. Matthews fought against the bloody mindedness of an old rose. But she won, scratched, torn and valiant. Dragging bags of compost out of the back of her car, swearing as her teeth rattled as her spade hit yet another stone, she had made progress in more than one way.

Peter, despite his gruffness, was an easy companion. Willing to fetch, carry and make her endless mugs of tea, accompanied by slices of what she suspected was a home-made cake. In turn, his neighbours found an excuse to be out in their front garden, the desolately pulling of a few weeds near their shared border had resulted in a larger conversation, more tea and far too much cake. Here sitting on a small wall, with the sun beating down on her dirty sweaty face Dolores felt happy. This is what she loved doing, being part of a community. It was the whole reason she had joined a band rather than as a solo artist. Her record company had begged her to move on, leave her friends behind her. But she hadn't wanted to go it alone. She loved her bandmates, still did. They had made it, made the money, the hits and had the houses, cars, and drug habits to match. For all that, all Dolores had ever wanted was a family, unable to have one of her own, her mission she felt was to create urban, town and village families, where people could be together in a self-supporting community. Of course, she realised shortly after, this was all fine until you added people to the mix, but experience, trial and error and sheer willpower had shown her what she could achieve.

During those weeks Ruth too had noticed a difference. People had started saying hello to each other as they met. Small carrier bags began to be exchanged. Ruth's earlier foray into giving was beginning to show its rewards. Dolores, ever generous had given her more plants and vegetable seedlings than she knew what to do with. Tentatively, she had stopped by a couple of houses, leaving a selection of both on the front doorsteps of those who had spoken to her or simply nodded in the street. Ted, she knew was already beginning to sell potting compost, trowels, watering cans and packets of seeds.

A sentence from Dolores last sermon still beat a tattoo in her ears. Both she and Ted had discussed it as they'd walked back from Church. "Mother Teresa," said Dolores had shown how that by one simple act of kindness nations could break down hatred, fear, and intolerance and that it wasn't the big extravagant acts of goodness that made the most difference, but small moments of kindness and that everyone should take these words to heart "If you can't feed a hundred people, then feed just one." And that was what they were trying to do now. OK, thought Ruth, her more so than Ted, who was cashing in on her plant giving initiative. Yet the shop was busier than it had ever been. He'd even allowed Maggie's useless excuse for a husband to start growing potatoes, beans, sprouts and tomatoes in his abandoned back garden. The motto was simple, when you have enough for your own use, give to those who haven't.

Not everyone had taken kindly to the new initiative, as Ruth herself had been pelted with a bag of spicy lettuces she'd left for the old bag at number 39. "I don't want your charity!" the old lady had screamed as she hurled leaves and radishes at Ruth. That tide had turned when the old woman had shouted at her a few days ago demanding that she wanted some of those potatoes she'd given to number 27. Resisting the temptation to hurl them at her, Ruth had struggled up the road with a large bag of freshly dug new potatoes, only to be told that there were far too many and she only wanted three for her supper.

It wasn't just in the people that the change was present once forlorn straggly gardens were beginning to perk up. People were out more, the summer instead of being a soggy one, shone brightly, encouraging people to take advantage of the warm light, and as the craze of patio parties began to filter down into the suburbs, gardening programmes began to create cost effective ways of enjoying the summer without it costing a fortune. Nectar to the residents of Hope Crescent whose underlying worries about the winter were already beginning to unfold.

Dolores noticed the difference. Her own home produce she used to make soups, Gavin who had suddenly found he had a gift for making bread and Mrs T's simple tray bakes were all added to her three days a week soup rounds. She'd advertised on the Church noticeboard that anyone who was struggling financially could apply to go on her soup register. It was nothing fancy, just a litre of soup, a loaf of bread and a what Mrs T feels like making cake. She couldn't give a definite answer as to what soup it would be. It's what I feel like on the day, she'd said on more than one occasion. Not caring for how many laws she was possibly breaking, the numbers had steadily risen to thirty.

"Who's going to pay for the additional ingredients" Gavin had asked exhaustedly one evening.

"I will. I've got it all organised." Pouring two brandies, she offered one to Gavin and taking the second flopped down on the sofa. They're struggling.

"So are lots of people. We're hardly rich ourselves." He grumbled, draining his drink, and wished he hadn't. He'd forgotten that Dolores liked Remy Martin and not the cheap stuff he occasionally bought at the pub.

"Help yourself" Dolores nodded her head towards the bottle. Today had been a difficult day. Two funerals and another parishioner had died from Covid complications. Despite reassurances, Covid's ugly presence still haunted and hunted the streets at night, the fear of the pandemic might be over, but the fear of freezing to death in an unheated house was becoming just as big a menace.

"All we can do is try. Look we have a knitting group now who are making blankets. We didn't have that six weeks ago."

"It's only because they can use the church hall and its warm in there, and you insist on letting them have decent coffee and cake. They'd be mad to go anywhere else!"

"Oh, don't be so bloody miserable." Dolores threw a cushion at him. "No seriously Gavin, we have to try and make a difference. We can't just administer to their souls; we have to help nourish their minds and bodies as well."

"It's going to cost a bloody fortune and other churches aren't doing it."

"They are. We all have to do our bit, and despite your grumpiness you are still going to make bread tomorrow morning, and love doing it. Or else!" Deftly catching the cushion Gavin threw back at her, they laughed, and drank the bottle dry before staggering up to bed. For once Dolores did not dream in music, the tree was calling out to her, waving its branches and as it did so, its fruit began to fall steadily to the ground. This was a message.

Ruth and Delores were having coffee in the vicarage kitchen, rain was thrashing against the windows. A late summer storm had been brewing for days, threatening clouds, lightning and thunder had split the sky in two. Dolores loved it, Ruth she felt, did not.

So, after braving the weather they sat at the old, scarred kitchen table. Dolores was making fruit pies, while Ruth peeled the fruit. Mrs T had gone to visit her sister for the day and Gavin was making his pastoral visits. Something, Dolores sneakingly felt he enjoyed. He invariably came back stuffed with cake, biscuits, and tea.

Watching the apple peel snake across her hand and wrist, both women worked in companiable silence. Despite her music background, Dolores hated listening to the radio, it annoyed her, the over jovial presenters, the way they laughed pretending everything was fine and fun in the world. Anyway, she'd always steered away from sugar pop or whatever they were playing today. She liked lyrics to mean something, to tell a story and not be about getting laid or making loads of money.

Gently rolling out the pastry, she stared at Ruth's blonde, grey head, bent studiously over the apples.

She had to ask.

"You alright, you seem a bit glum.  Nothing to do with Ted, is it?"

"No, I'm fine." Ruth's eyes remained fixed on the apple peel.

"OK." Smoothing the silky pastry onto the bottom of a plate, she glanced at Ruth again.  Give it time, she thought.  It wasn't until she was over by the cooker, stirring the first batch of raspberries, strawberries and redcurrants that Ruth began to speak.

"I don't want to talk about him."

"Fair enough. I always thought you two weren't that much of a match." She added goadingly, while still stirring the fruit.

Thumping the peeler on the table, Ruth hissed between her teeth, "he seems to think that he can tell me what to do.  I just about had enough of it with Harry, I don't want it from him."

"Can't be easy, for Ted I mean. He's worried about Maggie and Ian, Lesley's death cut him deep, and like the rest of us over fifties, he has no idea how to date or even ask someone out for a date anymore.  I mean the other week; some man came up to me while I was in Sainsbury's and said that he thought I looked good for my age and did I want to join him for coffee.

"And?"

"I did."

"You didn't!" Shocked, Ruth dropped the apple she was peeling.

Stooping to pick it up, Dolores casually said. "Course I did, any man who thinks he can pick me up with that line has really got it soooo wrong."

"What happened?"

"Well, he went on saying that he owned a yacht, and then proceeded to tell me that if I lost a bit of weight, he'd consider dating me full time."

"Bloody hell!" Exclaimed Ruth, nearly managing to slice her hand with the peeler in her astonishment.

"That's what I said. Oh, it gets better, he said that if I changed my clothes, wore a bit of makeup etc he could, possibly take me to a yacht club party. I think he really thought he was doing me a favour."

"What did you do?"

"Undid my cardie." Dolores sniggered evilly "you should have seen his face when he saw my dog collar. Oh, Ruth it was hysterical.  I've never seen a man get up so fast and bolt. It's a good thing." She tasted the fruit gingerly from an old teaspoon, pulling a face at its tartness, she poured a little more sugar into the mixture from an old glass jar standing on the work surface. "That I'm not easily offended. But it's not really good for one's ego to be referred to as an old bag lady."

Bursting into laughter both women enjoyed the moment.

"So, what has happened between you and Ted?"

"It was really nothing, he just said that he didn't like what I was wearing, it didn't" she snarled "do anything for me!" Ruth waited for Dolores to reply, and then realised that the other woman was too busy.

"I'm listening," added Dolores, spooning hot fruit into the pie bases.

"I suppose I just took it the wrong way.  I had spent hours getting ready and thought I looked good, and then for him to say that. I was a bit silly really, I told him to go home and that he wasn't that much of a catch himself.  Stupid, wasn't it?"

"Not really, but men I've noticed don't often think before they step into their mouth's. The boys were like it in the band.  They didn't mean it but some of the things they said could be hurtful and bloody disrespectful."

"Why did you give up?"

Dolores paused for a moment, her teaspoon hovering close to her lips. "I didn't really give up, I just thought it was time for me to leave. The band's still going, they've a new lead singer. I think she's the third one. No, it was time for me to leave, and I found that I had another calling, the Church. I wanted to do something more with my life. I'd been in the music business for thirty odd years, and I couldn't cope with the changes or the videos. They tried to get me crawling over men half my age. I wasn't so much a cougar more like an old crocodile, all teeth, snapping at young, tanned flesh, it was horrible. Oh, you can laugh" she added giggling "it was hell, I don't think the band saw it as sad! They were like yeah, get on with it and stop making a fuss! But it was fine for them to be swarmed over by a parade of skeletons with fake smiles, I just had the underwear ad boys. All gleaming smiles, hairless chests wearing budgie smugglers." Ruth let out a snort of laughter, and they both began to giggle uncontrollably.

"OK, so what is all this hilarity?" Gavin asked mockingly at the door. "After an afternoon with Mrs Haydock and her sister, I think I deserve to be in on the joke." Before either woman could stop him, he picked up a spoon and helped himself to a pie filling.

Rolling his eyes as he sucked the filling off the spoon, he smiled "Oh, heaven. I've eaten rock cakes that could have sunk the Titanic. Please tell me we are having one of these for dinner tonight." Throwing himself into a spare chair, he grabbed a handful of apple peel and began to nibble on one of the strands.

"Old Ted's a bit upset." He added, while finishing off a second strip of apple peel. "You two have a bit of a bust up?" He looked at Ruth enquiringly.

"He...he. Stumbling over her words, Dolores butted in for Ruth.

"He was being a bit of a pratt. Told her that he didn't like what she was wearing." Interjected Dolores as she began to trim the pie crusts.

"Brave or stupid? I can't decide." Added Gavin winking at Ruth.

"What would you have done?"

"Me?" Asked Gavin aghast.

"Yes you." Answered both women together.

"This is me you are talking about." Gavin rubbed his hands together, grinning at them. "I would have said that you looked lovely and then taken you shopping under the pretext of buying myself a new pair of jeans, and while we were there, we could look at something nice for you. Perhaps something other than grey, beige or brown."

Ruth's mouth fell open, tears threatened but instead of falling, they vanished under his impish grin. Chucking a handful of peel at him.

"Cheeky bast…"

"Hey, I am a curate, can't say those things to me." Laughing uproariously, he took Ruth's hand in his. "Don't be offended. But Ted is right, you do need some new clothes, I think he cares for you a lot. He seemed really down in the mouth when I popped in this afternoon. Why not go around. No, don't look like that," he retorted seeing her face turn mulish "tell him that he upset you, say that you only have earth tones in your wardrobe and that you would love to go shopping with him. I'll tell you this, he will either run a mile or actually be interested in what you wear." Patting her hand in his, he dropped his voice and casting a quick look at Dolores, added "he's not trying to control you. I think he's really proud of you, he just wants you to become yourself, and that's a lot more vibrant than you think you are. Think on it, please. You're two of my favourite people and I want to see you happy together."

Blushing heavily, Ruth asked "You really think so?"

"Wouldn't say it if I didn't believe it." Gavin added gruffly. "Right now, I've sorted out your love life I'm going out for a run and you women" he wagged his finger theatrically at them, "get on with your pie making, I want one when I get home."

"You'll be lucky."

Walking out of the kitchen, Gavin called over his shoulder "I damn well hope so!"

Chuckling as he made his way upstairs, Gavin thought of Ted. He'd been in a right state, complaining of how he had lost her, been so stupid. Gavin whose wife had left him when he'd told her that he was giving up his London financial practice to become a vicar had vowed to stay clear of love. That was why he loved living with Dolores, she was the same, her husband had left her because she couldn't have kids, so they were like an old married couple. An easy friendship, comradeship where no one was trying to get the upper hand. But a little matchmaking, yes bring that on, just because he didn't ever want to feel the pain and hurt, he'd been through, didn't mean that he didn't believe in love, he did. Just not for him.

Sitting in the kitchen Dolores realised that perhaps she was a little bored. So far, despite the odd deaths, tantrums, adultery and virtually every other sin under the sun, she wanted to do something different. She'd finished the song the night before and knew she could see it. Tom Wattingly was practically begging her to write something for some artist he was managing. The trouble was, she thought this was too good for her and not good enough for a top 10 hit. This song needed more, an older voice, a voice like hers.

Checking that the fiends weren't up to anything heinous like chasing next doors dog or mugging the chickens across the field from her, she grabbed her bag, coat, keys and dogs. She knew what she would do, she'd go home for the day. Just a day of rock star instead of being a parish north star.

Humming as she drove, the two dogs nestled down on the untidy back seat. Coats, shoes and at least two sweaters littered the seat and footwells, but Dolores didn't care. She'd seen that Gavin had had a decent car to drive, and that had become the church car. This one was hers, her personality, her things. Each mile closer to home, made her smile a little brighter.

Pressing the gate control, she stared up at the house, it was the only thing she had refused to give up. This was home, a sprawling farmhouse set within 12 acres of land. Too much for one person, her bandmates, as their marriages and partnerships dissolved had drifted to Sweet Chestnut Farm and under the pretext of staying a night, had moved in permanently. The house was now a group of ill-defined flats, everyone making their mark on their own piece of territory, she didn't mind. They paid the bills, looked after the house the gardens and the smallholding attached to it.

The papers she thought, as she stopped in front of the house, would have a fit if they knew that five rockers known for the larger-than-life image were just five normal people, wanting to live a quiet life away from the camara's and the press induced feuds. Mickey, the rhythm guitarist she knew would be gardening, Andy her lead guitarist would probably be working in the sanctuary.    Rescuing racehorses had become his passion, seeing animals treated as commodities had eaten away at his soul, and now, Dolores knew, he would be putting his hands at risk, retraining, and giving a new life to a horse that shortly beforehand had been staring at a slaughterman's crowbar.

Miles on the other hand, would be entombed in the loft with his model railway.  His wife had left him because of it. Most of the time, he only came out for meals or when the band needed to rehearse or tour.  Dolores had always thought of him as one of the best drummers around, but instead, like many other artists she knew, instead of showing off his talent he had withdrawn from the world and was quite happy expanding his rail empire through her loft.

That just left Phil, her bassist and best friend from school.   They'd been kicked out of the choir for smoking, and then begged to come back as their voices had blended and melted with each other's harmonies. They'd been together ever since. Phil, she knew would be working at the local junior school. He had become a part-time music teacher and taught everything from the recorder to bass guitar. The kids loved him, his unruly hair, twinkling eyes and energetic teaching methods. Phil was one of life's dads.

So, she thought, getting out the car and grabbing the dogs leads before they could charge across the front seat, she was home.

The house was silent, except for the grandfather clock in the hall. She had bought it from a sleazy second-hand place in Eastbourne and loved it. Like every other clock in the house, it didn't actually tell the right time, but that didn't matter, she loved its silky walnut finish, and deep sonorous tick tock. Letting the dogs off their leads, she pottered through into the kitchen, switched the kettle on, found a packet of biscuits in the tea caddy, of all places, and slumping gently into an old leather armchair next to the Aga, she sighed contentedly. Sometimes, you had to come home just to realise how lucky you were.

## Late Summer

Pacing up and down the village hall, Ruth bit the corner of her thumb in agitation. She could hear Dolores singing softly in the kitchenette through the clatter of cups rattling on saucers, and the rattle of teaspoons.

"Gardening Club" what on earth had made her suggest it, let alone try and organise it. Vaguely, she thought that the idea had stemmed from Dolores, she had laughed about her rose exploits with Peter, and the little group that had magically come together, proving that there was a need for solidarity and of companionship and that some sort of gardening club may be a good idea, to foster an interest in gardening and the local environment, which after a lot of thought, Ruth had asked to take on.

After all, why shouldn't it work? The affectionately known Snitch 'N' Bitch knitting circle was growing steadily, it was so named after the government had announced that people should report their neighbours if they thought they were using too many natural resources such as water or leaving too many lights on for too long. So now, despite the summer heat and squeaky needles, hats, scarves, blanket squares, and an array of wrist warmers were clicked, clacked and hooked onto needles or crochet hooks, with everyone enjoying the free electricity, the church was providing.

Ruth knew that Dolores had already been challenged on the sudden increase in the utility bills. Responding she had said that there was a need for community projects and had simply asked for a £1.00 donation towards the electricity, water, and refreshments. No one had complained, they hadn't dared to, after all it had been Dolores who had scoured the charity shops for bargain balls of wool, needles, hooks and easy patterns.

Watching Dolores lay out a dozen cups and saucers on a small table in the alcove, Ruth blurted out "Do you think anyone will come?" Her fingers plucking her cheek nervously.

Pausing to squeeze Ruth's arm gently, Dolores concentrated on her task, she could feel Ruth's anxiety "look even if no one else comes there will be you, me, and Ted. Doesn't mean we can't have a good natter and come up with some ideas. Give people time. And look at you! Four months ago, you were hiding in your house, too afraid to come out and now you are organising something that could really make a difference to the parish. You've grown so much, your clothes, hair and you are now the gardener you want to be. So, no matter what happens tonight, you can hold your head high. To be perfectly honest I do hope a few turn up as I have some news."

"You're not leaving are you!" Dolores could feel the panic before she saw the look of horror on the other woman's face. Her eyes widening as her right hand clutched her neck.

"No, but it will affect the community."

"What is it?" Ruth asked, her hand still clutching her throat.

"You'll have to wait." Snatching her head up, she stood stock still. Over the years she had developed an ear for reporters hiding behind cars, fences, and up trees, waiting desperately for a juicy story or even better a compromising photograph, and as such could detect the slightest movement. Smiling she reached out and gently spun Ruth around by her shoulders. "We're in business."

They trickled in nervously. Some people she recognised, others she had never seen before. Ted came in smiling, a quick easy word to all those he knew, a kiss on the cheek for Ruth, his touch on her hand and kiss demonstrating that she was more than just a friend to him. Dolores watched and smiled, Ted she realised, when he let his guard down was demonstrative and caring. On more than one occasion he placed his hand on the small of Ruth's back, giving her a smile, a nod and even a flirty wink. Dressed in jeans, checked shirt and boots, Dolores could see that Ruth was also doing him good, away from the shop and in her company, he flourished with natural attractiveness.

Dolores chatted easily to the Morrisons, the Patels and a couple with an unpronounceable surname called Aaron and Mumbuda, or Biddy for short. Massaging her temples Dolores realised that there were over 20 people in the room, all trying to get over their nervousness and connect with the people around them.

Looking at Ruth, Dolores motioned that she should leave them all to chat for a little longer and allow them to naturally settle down. Dams that suddenly broke could never be immediately blocked again.

Almost at once the crescendo of noise, broke into silence. Dolores, who was going to welcome everyone to the meeting, stood there, adrenaline coursing through her veins. She loved the feel, the moment when she would eventually step onto the stage.

"Welcome, and welcome to St. Matthews Village Hall and to the first gardening club meeting." Beaming she added "It's so good to see so many of you here and I hope that together we can foster a love of gardening and grow our community spirit." Grinning out at the audience as they clapped, she raised her hand to quieten them down "I am now going to hand you over to Ruth and ask you all if you have any ideas of how we can brighten our streets and create a better neighbourhood to speak out. I've also a little news, but I will leave that until the end. Ruth"

"Thank you, vicar," Ruth could feel her voice shaking in time with the backs of her legs. "Welcome and as the vicar said it is so good to see you all here tonight. I'm Ruth and I've only been gardening for a couple of months." A loud cheer came up from the back of the room, followed by several catcalls shouting, never, five months, ten years. Waiting for a momentarily break in the conversations that had suddenly sprung up like seedlings in the room, Ruth raised her voice "Following on from the Rev. Dolores I thought we could discuss how we could make our streets look better."

"Get the council to mow the green spaces." Shouted Mary James from number 12.

"Stop dogs from fouling the pavements." Biddy called from the back of the room.

"What about wilding some of the areas, like they are doing in San Francisco." Shouted another voice.

"Do what?" Called out Peter, who had sneaked in after the meeting had started.

"Re-wilding or wilding. People ride about on skateboards and sprinkle seeds on neglected urban spaces. It looks fantastic and it would also be beneficial for wild, insect and bird life."

"Can't see the council letting us do that" muttered Jim Campbell. "Probably say that someone could slip on a petal."

"But it's ok for us to slip in sh…"

"Yes, thank you." Butted in Dolores hastily "But it sounds a great idea. What do the rest of you think?"

Feeling a sense of purpose flow through her, Biddy stood up and asked "And we don't have to use council ground. We've all got patches of grass in front of our garden walls. Why can't we plant those and see what happens."

"That sounds great, what about the rest of you?" Ruth losing her shyness, grabbed a piece of chalk and wrote it down on an old blackboard Dolores had found rotting at the back of the shed.

Again, conversations volleyed around the room, only Peter could think of the hard work it was going to entail "So, who's going to do all this work. I can't not with my bad back." He muttered sullenly.

Leaning forward, Biddy tapped him on the shoulder "we can all do our own gardens." Then looking at her husband asked "unless our boys are prepared to help. They could scatter seed as they skateboard to school."

"Yes, but only on agreed areas, we can't do anything unless we have prior approval from the homeowner.

We can't afford to upset people, and some people just like square bits of lawn."

"Or weeds up to their windows," replied Alice Maundy tartly.

"OK, let's do one thing at a time. I take it most of you agree with the wilding project?" This time there was a hearty yes.

"Right Biddy, could you ask your two boys if they would like to help out. We need to find flour dredgers and we can fill those up, and basically your lads can sprinkle the seeds. However, they must know that we can only do this on permission given private land."

"What if there's some wind." Asked Ted cheekily.

A couple of people tittered.

"No, I'm being serious. What happens if the wind catches the seed and settles it on council land?"

"Or birds?"

Standing up, Dolores opened her arms "Well they would all be called acts of God. We are not responsible if God feels that the odd bit of council land needs a bit of colour, are we?" Squinting slightly and cursing herself for leaving her glasses in her study, she could feel them grinning with amusement. Had she just given them a charter to misbehave? Possibly, but hand on heart she had made sure that everyone understood what they had to do.

"Ted!"

Looking up in surprise, he could feel Dolores's eyes boring into him.

"How's the bartering system going?"

"Great"

"For those who don't know. Ted is coordinating our bartering system. This means that if you have any excess veg or fruits that are in sellable condition, Ted takes them on and exchanges them with a local farm who sells them on. In return we get eggs, homemade cheese and if we're very lucky homemade sausages."

"That's right. However, it does depend on what we're selling and the farm like to have a wide variety, not just lettuce and tomatoes. Each time you drop fruit or veg in, I weigh it and then, a bit like rationing you will receive the appropriate goods back, if you want them. There are already a couple of families who have donated all their bartered goods to either the soup service or have given items to needy families. All I will say is, this is illegal and therefore, you need to sign up to the system and not tell anyone else about it. Maggie's husband, Ian," his voice tightened at the very mention of the word "is also planting beetroot, potatoes, beans and getting the winter vegetables ready so we should have sprouts, parsnips, kale and I dread to think what else ready for later on in the year. If you want any seedlings, pop into the shop and put your name on the list and what you would like."

"Thanks Ted. I appreciate all your hard work and help. As Ted mentioned the soup service, I'll just say that we now have thirty-six people on our list, so if anyone does have any spare fruit or veg, which can't be sold but would be perfect for soups and pies to let me have it. With fuel prices rising, there are a lot of scared people in the area."

Several heads nodded and the room quietened down.

"What about your news vicar?" Mary added, helping herself to a biscuit at the back of the room.

"First of all, I just want to say thank you, not just for coming tonight, but for supporting Ruth's project and being so generous to Ted. I know it's early days, but we are doing something so worthwhile, and the more people we can get involved the better. However, I received a letter yesterday from Dillingby Council with regards to Witching's Field. It would appear that the council are considering selling the field to a local developer who wants to build two blocks of flats on the area."

Sitting down with an "Umph" Dolores waited, it was a full five minutes before the storm began to abate.

"They can't take it away from us." Growled Peter.

"It's been Witching's Field ever since 1423, it's protected!" Yelled a new voice from the back.

"Unfortunately, it's not! There are no precise details that any witches were executed on the spot." Rubbing her temples, Dolores waited for the noise to die down. "We have three options. The first is we do nothing and wait and see what happens, which basically means when the construction company move in, we won't be able to do anything except grin and bear the noise and welcome 130 new families to our community. Secondly, we try and find out why, and when it was called Witching Field, and see if we can save it as a heritage site and thirdly, and this is my preferred option, we turn it into a green space for the local community. If the council can see that we have tidied the area up, created gardens, paths and class it as a recreational area they may be persuaded to leave it alone. Also, I need to talk to a tree specialist. The chestnut tree is older than it looks and if it has a history and environmental importance, i.e. its fruit can be used to create authentic chestnut recipes such as liqueurs, breads, cakes, and tarts we may be able to raise local awareness and a petition to save the ground.

"Liqueurs?"

"Apparently so. I had a holiday in Madeira, they use sweet chestnuts in a lot of local produce. I thought we might be able to do the same. Perhaps even hold a fair later on in the year, highlighting their benefits as well as raising some money for the field's restoration."

"We've got to do something" cut in Peter. "I'm not having 130 people staring into my kitchen and bathroom every night."

"Same here!" Another voice rang out. Although their voices where loud Dolores could detect a hysterical undertone. They were suddenly afraid.

"So, I take it we are going to rule out option one." Shouted Ruth above the din of angry voices.

"Too damn right…. Oh sorry vicar, no offence meant." Called out Mary, her face glistening with anger and perspiration.

"None taken!"

"But we have to do something." Roared Ruth. Everyone immediately shut up. "I mean we cannot just sit back and do nothing; we have to think of something."

"Like what?" Peter called out, his fingers plucking anxiously at a loose fibre in his jumper.

"We could clean it up for a start." Added Dolores. She suddenly felt tired. The voices were becoming a bit of a blur. Too much time on her own she thought. "It's nothing more than a dumping ground for shopping trolley's, bicycle parts, dog crap and litter. We could start a clean-up operation, get the local media involved, tell them what we are trying to do. Could be a good general interest story and who knows who else may help us."

"Great!" Blood was coursing through Ruth's veins; she had never felt so angry in her whole life. Who in the hell were they to take away their field!

"What about asking the local junior school to help us. After all we do support them financially?"

"Good idea, but no." Replied Aaron. "Fifty years ago, it may have been possible but there is no way any school is going to risk being sued for allowing nine- and ten-year-olds to help us out. Can you imagine the compensation claims, if any of them were stung by a bee or cut themselves on a broken bottle. I'm afraid, if we want to save this land, we are going to have to do it ourselves."

"Maggie? Could you ask your husband?" Ignoring Ted's look, Ruth plunged on "could you ask him if he can get his hands on an industrial lawn mower and a couple of petrol strimmer's. We really need to clear the land to see what we've got. And, if we all clear a six-foot area in front of our back fences, we'll be able to get an idea of what we are dealing with and work inwards towards the tree. Aaron you're an architect, right?

"Retired!"

"Could you create a schematic drawing of the field."

"It's a rectangle Ruth," added Ted calmly.

"No, I mean if we have a proper drawing of the site, we can start to plan how we are going to create a garden. This way we can all look at it, make proposals and then agree on how we are going to move ahead. If not, it'll just be a hodge podge of all our ideas. We need to create something that will make these council people think again!"

Ruth looked up and caught Dolores's eye, winking back, Ruth suddenly had an odd feeling. An image of Dolores flashed through her mind reminding her of an Agatha Christie character; Mr Harley Quinn, he had never interfered but somehow through him, the truth was found, and Dolores was doing just that. She wasn't forcing them into anything but had known how to use the news to see if it would unite them or drive them apart.

Three days later and operation 'Wilding' came into force. Biddy and Aaron's sons Adam and Devon armed with flower dredgers filled with seed, whizzed up and down the neighbourhood, and according to Aaron a lot of other places in-between. The boys had initially shrugged their shoulders when asked to help out, but now with the influence of Drew Mattingdale, a blonde dreadlocked girl of about 15, whose skateboarding skills were 'awesome!' They suddenly became the Hope Crescent eco warriors. Drew who had forced the truth out of them, had thought it a brilliant idea, called on a couple of her mates, included the two boys, and now before and after school the local neighbourhood was dredged with seeds. She'd also been fascinated about 'Witching's Field."

For Drew, this was an adventure another way of escaping what she termed a boring existence. She'd seen Dolores a couple of times and hadn't really thought of her except for another old fuddy duddy in a dog collar. She'd called on the boys while Biddy was sitting down with a pile of old local history books. The boys had been out, but Drew asked if she could wait for them. The house a blend of Caribbean mystery and Muslim architecture had appealed to Drew who thought it so exotic from her own parents traditionally decorated house. Hot spicey colours mixed with cool blues and concentric patterns. It was homely and comfortable.

"What are you up to?" Casually sidling up to Biddy's overburdened kitchen table with her mug of tea, she touched one of the books "What's all this about?"

Pushing her glasses to the end of her nose, Biddy looked up at the assured blonde-haired girl "the council are thinking of selling Witching's Field to a construction company. Who knows what they will build on it," she lied. "I thought if I could find out about its local history, and perhaps find out anything of importance we may be able to stop them and save it."

"Yeah, but it's a dump!" Pulling a chair back, Drew dropped herself onto it, her eyes roving over the books.

"Yes, but it's our dump. We've already got an action plan on how to clear it and once we've done that, we're going to create a garden space for everyone. We've all started to do a little bit and providing it doesn't rain next weekend we've got a scrap metal merchant coming to take away all the metal, and then we'll find a way to get rid of all the other stuff. This way." Biddy's glasses wobbled and landed on her top lip "we will show them that we mean business."

Drew wasn't sure if she wasn't more fascinated by the story or the glasses. "Can we help?" Her tone was slightly less assured. "A couple of us have helped out with the seed sowing, I can ask around and see who's free."

Beaming, and finally pushing her glasses back onto her nose, Biddy thrust a book in front of her "you can start by looking up anything that has to do with witchcraft, burnings and any folklore around these parts."

"Surely it will just be easier to Google it?"

"Easier, perhaps but not so fascinating, books sometimes contain so much more, a hint a suggestion."

Looking at Biddy in fascination, Drew pulled the book towards her. Suddenly she felt part of something, sitting in this odd house, with Biddy and an old book. She grabbed the notebook and pen Biddy offered her and settled down to work.

While skating home later that night, she decided it was time to visit a library.

Dolores and Ruth were walking through Witching's Field. Blaze bumbling along made Dolores smile. No matter what was going on in and around her life, Blaze and her clumsiness always made her feel better. Lulu as always was attached to her leg by an invisible chord. Trotting along beside her, she felt safe and secure. Dolores had taught her a couple of simple head cues. Lulu was still afraid of loud voices and anxious when told off, so Dolores had worked a couple of simple ways to communicate with her when walking. It worked.

Neither woman spoke, it was that type of friendship. Sometimes words were just an overlay, a patter of nothingness. Slowly, as if by some unbroken agreement they ambled gently towards the tree. Both wondering how on earth they were ever going to get the place cleaned up in a single weekend.

Standing under the tree, they drew breath. It was a warm muggy day, clouds lay languidly in the sky, it was one of those days where you didn't know quite what to do. The grass already yellowing in the heat flopped around their feet like gasping fish. Ensnaring and tangling your feet. Blaze huffing and puffing with the heat, threw herself down under the tree and panted. Lulu, following suit sat down beside her. Funny thought Dolores, that Lulu was the protector, the blind dog guiding her seeing friends.

Looking up Dolores gazed in wonder at the tree. How long had it been there, what had it seen, what stories could it tell. Would it have seen those poor deluded women screaming in agony as the fires caught hold. Had the tree felt their fear, panic, and pain. Would it have trembled alongside the victims. Who knew? Placing her hand against the bark, she could feel the warmth of the day vibrating through her hand. Staring up into its leafy canopy the leaves were just beginning to turn, heralding a new era in the tree's life. Its fruits were beginning to swell, the promise of a new bumper harvest.

A harvest that the newly formed, Mother's weekly group had their eyes on. Having shown them several recipes from an old Madeiran cookbook she had bought from the local church, the women had poured over the chestnut cakes, liqueurs, and salted baked chestnuts, deciding that this harvest they were going to create a harvest festival supper, which would include all things chestnut and whatever else they decided to bake.

Smiling at the thought, Dolores lent against the tree trunk. It's strength reminding her that even she, occasionally needed someone to lean on. She liked its silent warmth. Nearly jumping out of her skin as Ruth uttered a short, petrified scream.

"What is it?" Staring Ruth's white face, she repeated herself again "what is it?"

Shaking, her hands clutching at Dolores sleeve she uttered, "a snake, there was a snake, where your hand was. It was looking at me!"

Snatching her hand away from the trunk, Dolores took a step back and peered at the spot where her hand had been. "There's nothing there." She traced the bark with her fingertips. "However, it could have been the light, if you look the bark is twisted and gnarled." Looking into Ruth's petrified face she said "Don't be afraid. There's nothing there. I'll show you.  Place your hand where mine is, it's just bark and moss."

Cautiously, Ruth stretched out her hand, waiting to be bitten.  Disappointment coursed through her veins when her fingertips nervously touched knotted bark, and damp moss."

"Oh!" Her fingers, stronger now, traced the lines and cracks living within the wood.  "I could have sworn…."

"It's a funny day today and the light is different.  Could explain it. Don't you like snakes?"

Ruth shook her head "I don't, actually I have never seen one live before so I can't really say if I like them or not.  You?"

"Not so keen on the venomous ones, but your average snake, yes.  I went to a funny little zoo in Penang, where the owner let me hold a Python, it was only a young one and he told me how to hold it.  It was an amazing experience.  She was so vibrant, strong, and alive.  From then on, I've never really worried about them."

"But the bible, surely?"

Dolores thought for a moment, her eyes still staring into the leafy canopy and softly asked, "can you keep a secret?"

"You know I can."

"Well, I've always had a problem with the snake in the garden of Eden. God promised Adam and Eve that they would not be bitten, stung, or harmed by any of the creatures living in the garden. So, if that's the case, how did the snake get in. If they were so protected, how did he or she break their defences, and snakes have suffered ever since for it. Yet within the Book of Genesis, we see that snakes are seen as protectors and healers which is why they are now a symbol of healing when intertwined with the staff. And if you believe more pagan ideas then you would know that all trees have guardians, and these can take all forms. So perhaps this tree has survived for so long because it has a guardian. Whatever, it is, it will not hurt us, and perhaps," she added with a snigger of devilment, "if we can't find enough information to save the field, we'll have to come up with a bit of folklore to keep this place alive. Come on, I'll be late, and I promised Gavin that I would go to the movies with him tonight." Calling for Blaze, she deftly clipped her lead on, and the two women walked towards the communal gate.

Before parting, Dolores reached out for Ruth's hand "Don't worry about what happened back there." Nodding her head to one side she looked into Ruth's troubled eyes "the world is filled with things we don't understand. Just think of it as a benign spirit. See you tomorrow, Gavin's dragging me off to a Thor movie."

"Thor?" Ruth's amazement rang out on the still air. "Thor!"

"Yeah," Dolores beamed back at her "good looking, a bit thick and plenty of action. Celibacy can be harder than you think." She added sniggering. Hugging each other, Dolores left Ruth by the gate. She was looking forward to an evening of testosterone and bulging muscles.

Ruth woke at six, Ted lay fast asleep beside her. She was surprised that it had taken him so long to suggest that he stay over, and yet it had felt so magical. Laying in the languid warmth of the bed, she snuggled down closer to him, sliding her arm across his waist. It was a whole new experience, she could feel his warmth, closeness, whereas Harry had felt like a plank of wood when she'd tried to curl up beside him, shaking her off, saying that she made him feel hot. Another hour, another hour and then it was 'D' day. But for now, she was in no hurry as she felt an unusual peace steal over her.

Peace was in short supply at the vicarage, Dolores swore as she marched from the greenhouse to the potting shed, 'what the hell had she done with her secateurs? She knew she had put them down somewhere.' Knowing that she didn't need them for the great clean up wasn't helping her mood. Savagely she blamed the cats, that was it, they had moved them to spite her.' Her mood dissipated as Madge, shot out from the bushes, ambushing her legs before streaking across the lawn with her tail waving in the wind. Roaring with laughter, Dolores immediately felt better, Squirrel and Verity shot out of their hiding places after her. Rough and tumble on the lawn while the dogs snoozed in a spot of sunshine. Grateful that they were being left alone for five minutes. Furry dogs made perfect snoozing posts and Dolores felt a stab of pity for the two girls as the three fiends used them mercilessly for their own selfish and comfortable needs.

Looking down she spied her secateurs lolling in a pot of petunia's. Of course, she'd been deadheading them yesterday afternoon. Grabbing hold of them before she lost them again, she slipped them in her pocket and wandered back into the house. Time for one more cup of coffee before she left.

Ted had drawn up an action plan, dividing the field into manageable quarters he waited nervously for everyone to arrive. The late summer sun was poking her head out from behind the clouds, warming his back. Double checking his list, he felt Ruth's soft lips brush his cheeks.

"Stop worrying. People will come."

"Trouble is that what people say and what they do are usually two different things. I just want it to be a success for you and Dolores. You've worked so hard to get things going."

"Whatever happens it will always have been a success, look at what we have achieved. We have a knitting group, Mother's Weekly, and a gardening club, people are gardening, growing food, sharing that food. In the last six months we have begun to grow as a community. People stop and chat in the street, we meet up and have coffee at the Lemon Tree. Things have changed, Ted and for the better." Reaching up and touching his face, Ruth's smile softened "and I met you. The most wonderful thing that could have ever happened to me." Kissing her hand softly, Ted's eyes twinkled.

"Same here..." He was stopped from saying anything else as Drew, Biddy, Adam, Aaron and Devon noisily shouted their greetings. Waving to them, Ruth and Ted made their way across the field to meet them.

"I take it we are the first?" Asked Biddy, who's orange, pink and brown leggings and matching top suddenly brightened up the drab, browning field.

Within minutes the rest of the gang arrived, leaving only Gavin and Dolores to bring up the rear.

"Nice dreads," commented Dolores casually when she was introduced to Drew. "I had them once, whereas you look cool, I looked....."

"Amazing" Drew wanted to give her a hug but fought against it only to find her arms flapping like an irate goose.

"No, I looked like some down and out, and before you laugh. I remember I was standing outside Woolworths, the band, we had had our first top ten hit, we were in at number three, and I couldn't believe it. I wanted to go in and look at the singles, see where we were. Anyway, I'm standing outside trying to pluck up the courage to see it all for myself when this guy comes up and gives me a quid. Told me where I could find a bed for the night and to buy myself something to eat."

Looking perplexed at Dolores, Drew asked "you were in a band?"

"When I was younger. I was the singer and occasional guitarist." Smiling into the Drew's doubting eyes she smiled "it was all a long time ago. Both appearances and dreams change. You'll find that out for yourself one day."

Grabbing the bag that Gavin waved at her, Dolores let the past settle down, she couldn't believe that she still found it hard that people didn't believe that she had been a singer in a band. Unbidden, her new song, 'City of Angels' floated into her mind. She had been up half the night finishing it off. Now she needed to decide what she was going to do with it. Keep it for herself or sell it. Unlike most other songs, she found herself becoming more and more attached to it.

Working alongside Biddy and Gavin she was one of the advance parties. Their job was to pick up litter, broken bits of fencing, metal, or anything small and if and when they found something too big or heavy to go in their sacks they shouted to Neil, a man of about thirty with sharp rat like eyes and a dodgy moustache. Within the first hour they had found four bicycles, a car door, locked suitcase and a couple of knives. Looking at the finds Dolores thought that they hadn't started the tidy up a moment too soon. The last thing this neighbourhood needed were the nearby gangs taking out their grievances on one another behind their houses. They were just coming out of their shells and Dolores did not want the local residents scared again.

"I know you?" Devon's voice ripped through the still quiet air. Standing with a rake in his left hand, and rubbing his nose with his forefinger, he looked at Dolores. "Uncle Javid has an album of yours, you were with that strange band, 'Horseman apc.'"

"Horsemen Apocalypto!"

"That's right."

"But you're not one of the horsemen. You're Hope, well you are on the 'Devil May Care' album."

"Yes, I am. We decided that the original bands name, 'The four horsemen of the apocalypse and Hope' was too much of a mouth full, so we just called ourselves

Horsemen Apocalypto. I remember the album, the artwork, ahhhhh that artwork, it was out of this world!" she added dreamily. "I remember meeting Brian at a pub in Shoreditch, he was only about 20, but his style. He said that he loved the group and wanted to do something special. 'Devil May Care' was our second album, and probably the most successful, and there we were, the lads as the horsemen – death, disease, famine and pestilence all riding black horses and there was me, in white and gold shining like a star. Crazy times." Smiling at Devon, she said simply "say hi to your uncle Javid for me."

Speechless, Devon's mouth opened a little wider.

"You wrote Shake them Up and Bring me down, didn't you?" Demanded Drew, moving forward hesitantly.

"Well, the band wrote it."

"Yes, but it's being used for a car commercial."

"Not my voice though, I think Lydia performed on this one. She's the group's latest singer." Added Dolores slowly. She told herself that she didn't really mind, mind not being the star performer of the group. But she did. Stupid really. Bending down she picked up a couple of old coke cans. Anything to take the focus off herself. Drew she realised was watching her. Gazing briefly into her eyes, Dolores, felt her lips quiver into a smile. Why did she have to miss the band so much when it had been her decision, and hers alone to leave.

The tree she thought had echoed her inner tears, as the fruits growing in their spiny thorns began to descend, gently at first and then it was like the tree sneezed, shook its branches and an avalanche of sweet chestnuts rained to the ground.

"What are we going to do with them." Yelled Biddy from across the field. "We can't just let them rot." Turning swiftly, she located her sons who were busy talking to Neil, laughing at a couple of ancient TVs found in a hedge. "Boys, when you've finished that, get a couple of bags, and start picking the fruit. Jenny across the road from us says that has a sweet chestnut vodka recipe that she wants to try out.

"And don't forget the Mother's Weekly lot" yelled Dolores, "They'll skin me alive if they don't get any. They've got big plans for this little lot."

Ted's roar of laughter, bounced like the afternoon sunlight across the field. "Have you ever tried anything that Jenny has tried to make. Did anyone ever try her damson gin. Best drain cleaner I ever sold, even now people ask me if I have any left." A few cackles of laughter rang out in the air.

With the sun cooling, Dolores decided it was time they all had a break and invited them back for soup, bread, and cheese at the vicarage. They'd been working solidly for five hours, even Neil's truck looked near to breaking point. All that was left to do now was strim and cut the grass and Ian and a couple of his friends had said that they would come in and do it for them.

Just ever so slightly relieved that the work was almost over, Dolores tottered home to warn Mrs T that they were all on their way. Walking past the tree she saw the snake, turning its mottled brown head ever so slightly, a yellow eye, the shade of sunlight, glanced at her, winked before its eyelids closed blocking out its golden stream of light.

Standing stock still, Dolores caught her breath. It was time. She hadn't thought it would come this quickly. Pretending that she had lost something she stared amongst the tree's roots. Nothing yet. It was obviously a warning. Stifling back a sudden tear, she walked resolutely on. Hands pushed down deep into her pockets she told herself off for being silly. She knew the rules, but somehow, here among these people she had felt at home, felt she belonged.

Sighing with relief as she walked up the vicarage path, she realised that nothing would happen until the spring. If she was sensible, she'd get on with the harvest festival and party and enjoy the time she had.

"You never told us how your meeting went with Mark Foster went at the council?" Asked Aaron as he helped himself to another serving of soup. They were all sat around the kitchen table while the youngsters had taken themselves off to sit in the conservatory, amid whispering and eye rolling.

Sighing slightly, Dolores cut herself another piece of cheese. "About as helpful as a damp dishcloth, he didn't know anything about the field except that it was council property, and that they saw a way of making money from it. He basically told me that I should be grateful as it would mean I could get a few more desperate souls coming to church."

"Ouch!" Cried out Ruth "That hurts."

"Not as much as it would if I hadn't had my dog collar on. All I could do was imagine my hands around his throat while his nasally little voice droned on. No, we have got to find another way. He's just looking at the money. Doesn't care less about the area or the people. So no, we are going to save the field ourselves and today has been a great help. Yes, it is going to look a little untidy, even after they've cut the grass, but the ground is damp, so we could start our wildlife seeding tomorrow if anyone's free. It'll only take me an hour to put out all the markers.

Unknown by the other's Drew was leaning against the door.  Suddenly she felt angry, angry that nameless people could just take something away, something they never knew they needed until recently "I may be able to help" she added conversationally, as she moved towards the stove and ladled another spoonful of soup into her bowl. Grabbing a slice of bread, turning it over in her hands she said.

"I haven't managed to find out that much about witches, but Witching's Field was used by 1930's serial killer John Gaston as his hunting ground.  Rumour is that he murdered twelve women from 1932 to 1935.  He used his looks and charm to lure young women out into the field.  I won't go into details, but all I can say is that it's the stuff of nightmares.  Anyway, they found the bodies of five women but not the rest."

"Yes, but surely the fields been dug over several times, they would have found the bodies." Demanded Aaron looking up over his spoon.

"Apparently not!" Drew sat down at the table "He refused to tell anyone where they were.  The locals took the law into their own hands and strung him up on one of the tree's branches. They said he laughed all the way to the noose.  Surely, we can protect the field with this. Even if it's not consecrated it could still or was a burial ground, and the tree. Well that now has history written all over it.

"There's something else," added Adam as he walked into the kitchen, placing his bowl carefully in the kitchen sink. Even if we can't protect the ground because of the killings, I reckon that tree is really old. Older than what most chestnut trees grow to."

Ruth shut her mouth, and let the spoon hover tantalisingly in front of her nose "what do you mean?"

"Most chestnut trees live to 150-200 years, this one by my calculations is around 500 years old."

"How did you find that out?" Asked Peter querulously.

"Easy, I measured the trunk and then multiplied it by 2.5. The trunk is about 2 metres."

"So, we could try and protect it as a piece of local natural heritage." Ruth added slowly. They all looked at Dolores who was sneakily feeding Lulu a piece of cheese under the table.

"It's OK, I am listening. Actually, you have all got something. It's illegal to erect a building on consecrated and non-consecrated burial plots. Now I know these women were killed and buried illegally, but I think the law would be the same. We've just got to prove what happened here and fight for their justice. Besides, not many people want to live on top of a graveyard. We're still so afraid of ghosts, so we can also use this as a backup plan. But first of all, we need as much information about the John Gaston killings as we can. Reasons he used the field. What was here in 1932, what it did to the locals. We need everything we can get our hands on.

Adam, can you look at the tree again. Can you try and find out if there is someone on the local environmental office who knows anyone who can confirm the age of the tree. If we have something unique, then we may just be able to use it."

Ruth's voice was husky with emotion when she spoke "but what about the field, I can't get it out of my head that there may be seven murdered women lying there. Can't we do something?"

"Well unless we dig the whole field up or get the council in to do it, I don't think there is anything we can do. When did they last look for the missing women, Drew?" Getting up Dolores grabbed a piece of paper from the dresser in the corner of the room. Shaking her pen, she started to write.

Husky with emotion, Drew took a deep breath, "I think the last time anyone checked was in 1974. Ethel Bradbury was his last victim and her mother tried to get the police to look for her daughter one last time before she died. She was convinced that she was buried in the field. From what I've read, the police made a half-hearted attempt, and said that they had nothing new to tell her, she died a week later.  Must have broken her heart not being able to find her daughter after all that time."

"Makes the whole place a bit creepy now" added Biddy with a shudder.

Dolores thought for a moment.  She could feel their sadness and fear. "I think we need to carry on as before. Create the garden, create something beautiful so that if they are still there, they are buried in a place of grace and beauty. We can't save them, and they can't hurt us, but perhaps we can help each other.  If there are no living relatives left, we can leave them in peace, and instead of shunning the place, why not make sure that we all use it, utilise it."

"Ian said he would make us a couple of benches from pallets, decent like." Stuttered Maggie, not daring to look at her father, "we could name each bench after the victims.  That way their names live on," Blushing she dropped her eyes back to the table.  Dolores had noted that Maggie was the quietest of the bunch, but when she did speak.

"What a wonderful idea and then at a later date if we can afford to buy proper benches, we can rename them. I think that's lovely.  Who's in agreement with me that we now really look after that field and keep the developers out." The cheers startled the dogs who leapt out of their beds and into the hall, and Dolores, rummaging around in the cupboards found a bottle of brandy.

That evening, the vicarage became the nosiest place for miles.

## Autumn

Autumn was beginning to settle in, a few fine days lifted the now threatening winter skies. Work on the field and the surrounding gardens, increased as harvests were brought together. All those who had wanted chestnuts had taken their share, neighbours shared produce with those around them and on the surface, everything seemed to be the same. Except, except that there was an air of expectation, as if everyone was waiting for something to happen.

Dolores loved harvest festival, the way the church felt and smelt. The new flower ladies had decorated the church with flowers, fruit, and vegetables, all of which were going to be used for pies and soup in the next batch of the soup run. She also felt more at peace, even when walking through Witching's Field. There was no menace there, the rubbish and filth had caused that, not the souls who'd perished. Ian had been as good as his word and mowed the field once a fortnight, just to get the grass under control and maintain some sort of order.

The borders had been dug over and after their boozy first night success they had come out again on mass and planted nearly three thousand bulbs ranging from snowdrops, which were sited under the tree, daffodils of all colours and sizes, formal borders of tulips and crocus, which they'd scattered so that they would form drifts of miniature colour. The new meadow beds had been sown and the builders had been in to lay the paths. They'd decided against muddy grass paths and chosen simple paving slabs. A series of fundraising events had financed the building works.

Walking across the field now, Dolores could hardly believe her eyes. A piece of waste ground had become a masterpiece in the making. Even the roped areas showing where plants had been planted or sown gave the area a finished look, while roses, donated from a closing garden centre now hinted at a promise of what was yet to come as they nestled against garden fences, re-energising for next years. She wasn't alone either, dog walkers pottered along the new paths, joggers had immediately made use of the outside circular track, even Ian's rustic benches were in demand as neighbours, making use of the mild weather walked, sat, and chatted.

This year's harvest festival was to be different. After the church service, and providing the rain held off, it had been agreed that they would celebrate it with a harvest lunch in Witching's Field. There would also be a special ceremony, a ceremony of peace for the departed, a celebration of the food they had grown and most importantly a celebration of a community that like the gardens around them, had grown and learned to support one another.

This year the church bells sounded fuller and vibrant. The service had been of hope, of the understanding of winter and the new promise that spring always brings.

People, plates and voices jostled with the heavily laden tables for space. They were hungry. Dolores had led a candlelit pilgrimage around the field, her voice light and uplifted as she offered prayers for the departed and for all that they had been given.

Dolores grinned when Drew, Adam and Devon asked if they could join in. It was an odd friendship thought Dolores, Drew was a flame which they both followed, she only hoped that only one of them would be in love with her. She would hate to see the boys end up hating each other. Yet, she thought Drew understood what was happening and had pulled back slightly. She went out with them less but spent more time with Biddy as they worked to uncover the fields secrets.

"Speech, speech" voices boomed like cannons as Dolores had stood up.

Waiting for them to calm down, she looked around her "Thank you, all of you thank you. You have no idea how humble I feel in your presence, when I look at you, I know that something magical has been created through your trust in one another. And although I could go on for hours, I only have one major thing to tell you and that is, Dillingby Council have contacted me, confirming that after the tree specialists reports, and thank you to Adam and Devon for working so hard on this, our tree is considered to be a rare and unusual species of chestnut, and as such, they are placing the tree and the surrounding area on the councils protected list. Drew, I also want to thank you for what you've done. Your school awareness campaign I've been told has been a great success. For those who don't know, Drew and Biddy created a 'Be Safe, Stay Safe' awareness programme at her local school. John Gaston preyed on the young and the vulnerable and Drew wanted to create something that would honour those who died by his hand and help girls in the future. So can I have a massive round of support and applause for Drew, Adam and Devon." Clapping thunderously, the three looked slightly shocked as Biddy and Aaron drew them into a group hug. Waiting for the noise to abate, Dolores finished by saying "Witching's Field is safe and all I ask is that we continue to look after it, nourish it and protect it for future generations to come. We are a community, let nothing break this wonderous new beginning." Wiping away the tears from her eyes, Dolores felt herself consumed as they all hugged each other. And out of the corner of her eye, there by the chestnut tree was a small sapling. She knew what it meant, but for now…. Right" she yelled above the sea of heads, the Mother's Weekly group have made chestnut surprise, chestnut cake and I believe that Jenny has a very young chestnut vodka on the go. So come on everybody, let's go chestnut."

The lunch drifted raucously into the night, at about midnight, Dolores moved silently over towards the tree. Offering a silent prayer as tears trickled down her face she reached out to the sapling. She could only ignore it for so long.

Rushing around to the vicarage the next morning, Ruth's mouth flew open and snapped shut when she saw Gavin at the door.

"She's not here" he answered softly to her enquiring gaze.

"Can I wait for her?" Gavin smiled and motioned for her to come in. "No, Ruth, I mean she has gone. It looks like she packed her bags last night and left. They've all gone, the dogs, cats, piano and her books."

"Gavin!" Ruth laid her hand softly on his arm.

"Oh," smiling ruefully, he added "I think I knew it was going to happen like this. When I came here, I didn't want to stay with her, I felt that her religious metre was so different from my own. But you know what? She taught me about God and humanity and how we cannot survive without each other. What she did, was prepare me for this parish."

"You?"

"Yes, I am to be priested at Christmas, and this will be my first parish as a vicar."

Throwing her arms around him, Ruth pulled him close and hugged him "that's fantastic news. You will be so great. I don't know what to say, except"

"You'll miss her, we all will, but I suppose she came here to do a job and now that she'd done it."

"But to not say goodbye..."

"She did, well sort of last night at the party. When she drank a toast to us all, I had a feeling then that she was saying goodbye. I just didn't expect it to be quite so quick. But Viv said that when she arrived, she did so at the dead of night. So perhaps that is just her way."

Looking down at Ruth's tearful face he returned her hug.

"She's left something for you."

"For me?"

"Yes, wait there I'll get it for you."

A minute or two later, Gavin reappeared carrying a parcel. "It's for you and Ted."

"What is it?"

"Well looking at the paper I would say that it is a wedding present."

"But! But he didn't ask me until after the party."

"Well Dolores, obviously thought that it was on the cards. And I hope you'll get married here. I can't wait to say that you are the first couple I married."

Laughing between their tears they hugged each other again, grasping the parcel to her chest, Ruth bumbled her way out of the house, tears running down her face.

Dolores switched off the ignition and relaxed for a second. A motorway café, she was dying for a mug of coffee and a bacon sandwich. The cats were still sleeping in their crate, Snapping leads on both Blaze and Lulu, she took them out to stretch their legs and a piddle. Inside, on the back seat her books, clothes and piano wrapped around each other for support and warmth. While in the front footwell sat a newly planted Sweet Chestnut tree, wrapped round its soft trunk snored a tiny snake, Bathdaisa, she wouldn't wake up until the spring.

It wasn't until she reached the car that she recognised the tall man lolling against it. Seeing her his smile brightened.

"Thought I might catch you here. The boys, well the boys want to know how you are fixed?"

"Why?"

"Cos we've got a gig on Saturday, interested?"

"Could be, I take it you are all at home?"

"None other! You'll do it?"

"Try and keep me away, besides I have a little time before I start my next job. Would be good to be all back together again. And" she added with a twinkle in her eye "I have a new song!"

"I thought you might!" Phil aka Death, helped her put the dogs back into the car. "Thought we could talk about the set over a cuppa." Slipping his arm through hers, he pulled her closer to him "Don't tell the boys this, but I think your new song." He looked around him theatrically, his black coat swirling across his legs "think we may have a new hit on our hands." Wrapping his arm around her shoulder, he muttered softly. "Hungry?"

"What do you think?"

Halfway across the car park Phil stopped suddenly, "by the way, Dennis phoned, he said that tatty piece of land you wanted to buy, it's yours."

Biting her bottom lip, Dolores laughed "Brilliant!"

"Going to tell me about it?"

"Might do, providing you buy me a burger."

Chuckling Phil let his arm drop, squeezed her hand, and slowly hand in hand they walked across the remainder of the car park in silence. Smiling to herself, Dolores thought, she might have a talent for writing slutty little songs for pop princesses. And, one thing she had learned as a vicar, if you want something to thrive, threaten to remove it. Nice of Mark at the council to lend her some paper.


Two trees were planted in Eden, the Tree of Knowledge of Good and Evil, and the Tree of Life, yet in an otherwise forgotten corner, was a space designated for a third tree, the Tree of Hope. And as God watched his creation disobey his rules, he realised that mankind were the only ones who could plant the third tree.

Humans were the only creatures, he realised, that needed Hope, so instead of banishing it, he allowed it to become an internal tree, a tree that could sustain mankind through some of their darkest hours. All humans needed was hope, and to find it within themselves.

Yet aware of the fragility of his people, he allowed the seeds of hope to fall, to be guarded by a select few, whose knowledge would be passed down through the generations, allowing Hope to spring up wherever and whenever she was needed.

Hope, God reasoned, could come in all sorts of shapes, sizes, and people.

**About the Author**

Samantha took to writing seriously when the roof on her house started to leak! Writing a monthly column about her 'Tales from a hovel,' she recounted her life living in a derelict house on the side of a mountain in Madeira.

After writing for several tourism newspapers and a news blog, as well as murder mysteries for a local amateur dramatic society, she finally decided to write a book, this one in fact, two weeks before a competition deadline.

She now lives in comparative luxury in a non-leaky flat in Madeira where she looks after her elderly pony, writes, gardens, practices Qi Gong and loves being a Wedding Celebrant.

Life is anything, but dull!